Dear Parent:

Congratulations! Your child is taking the first steps on an exciting journey. The destination? Independent reading!

STEP INTO READING® will help your ⬚⬚⬚⬚⬚⬚⬚⬚ 's five steps to reading success. Each step includes ⬚⬚⬚⬚⬚⬚⬚⬚ ⬚t. There are also Step into Reading Sticker Books, Step into Reading Main Readers, Step into Reading Write-In Readers, Step into Reading Phonics Readers, and Step into Reading Phonics First Steps! Boxed Sets—a complete literacy program with something for every child.

Learning to Read, Step by Step!

Ready to Read Preschool–Kindergarten
• big type and easy words • rhyme and rhythm • picture clues
For children who know the alphabet and are eager to begin reading.

Reading with Help Preschool–Grade 1
• basic vocabulary • short sentences • simple stories
For children who recognize familiar words and sound out new words with help.

Reading on Your Own Grades 1–3
• engaging characters • easy-to-follow plots • popular topics
For children who are ready to read on their own.

Reading Paragraphs Grades 2–3
• challenging vocabulary • short paragraphs • exciting stories
For newly independent readers who read simple sentences with confidence.

Ready for Chapters Grades 2–4
• chapters • longer paragraphs • full-color art
For children who want to take the plunge into chapter books but still like colorful pictures.

STEP INTO READING® is designed to give every child a successful reading experience. The grade levels are only guides. Children can progress through the steps at their own speed, developing confidence in their reading, no matter what their grade.

Remember, a lifetime love of reading starts with a single step!

*To Greg and Mark—my sparring partners,
board holders, and number one cheerleaders.
And to Mary Anne, my TKD comrade.
—T.P.*

*For Alison and the lillle one.
—T.B.*

Text copyright © 2006 by Terry Pierce. Illustrations copyright © 2006 by Todd Bonita.
All rights reserved under International and Pan-American Copyright Conventions. Published
in the United States by Random House Children's Books, a division of Random House, Inc.,
New York, and simultaneously in Canada by Random House of Canada Limited, Toronto.

www.stepintoreading.com

Educators and librarians, for a variety of teaching tools, visit us at
www.randomhouse.com/teachers

Library of Congress Cataloging-in-Publication Data
Pierce, Terry.
Tae kwon do! / by Terry Pierce ; illustrated by Todd Bonita. — 1st ed.
    p.   cm. — (Step into reading, step 1)
SUMMARY: Easy-to-read, rhyming text describes a tae kwon do class, at which children learn to
kick, punch, and spin, as well as to cooperate and have fun.
ISBN 0-375-83448-6 (trade) — ISBN 0-375-93448-0 (lib. bdg.)
[1. Tae kwon do—Fiction.   2. Martial arts—Fiction.   3. Stories in rhyme.]
I. Bonita, Todd, ill.   II. Title.   III. Series: Step into reading. Step 1 book.
PZ8.3.P558643Tae   2006   [E]—dc22   2005001304

Printed in the United States of America   First Edition   10 9

STEP INTO READING, RANDOM HOUSE, and the Random House colophon are registered trademarks
of Random House, Inc.

STEP INTO READING®

STEP 1

TAE KWON DO!

by Terry Pierce
illustrated by Todd Bonita

Random House 🏠 New York

We dress.

We go . . .

... to Tae Kwon Do.

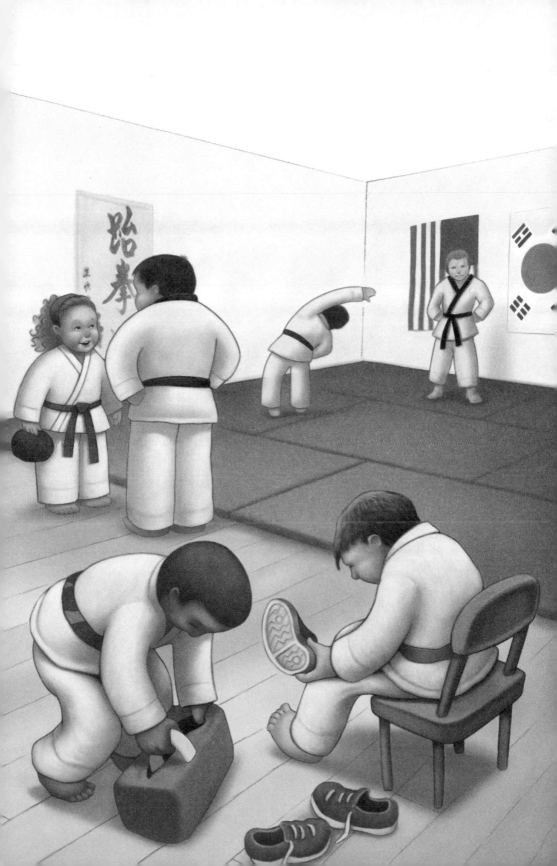

We stand.

We bow.

We step in now.

We jump.

We run.

We have some fun.

We count.
We yell.

We all kick well.

We hit.

We chop.

We fall.

We flop.

We look.

We pick.

We spin.

We kick.

The kick is good.

I bust the wood!

We box.

We jab.

We laugh.

We gab.

We stand.

We bow.

What fun.

Oh, wow!

Now we go.

"Bye, Tae Kwon Do!"